The Adventures
of Jessica
and Zebedee

Story by Linda Jay

CHAPTER ONE

Jessica frowned anxiously at the notice on the pet shop window. Scrawled in big, white letters were the words

**CLOSING DOWN SALE —
MASSIVE REDUCTIONS —
EVERYTHING MUST GO.**

From the look of the dusty windows everything had already gone. There was no sign of the squirming puppies or the bright, chirping birds that had been there a week ago.

Jessica pushed open the door and hurriedly made her way past the empty boxes and loose straw. At the back of the shop a large red and blue parrot was swinging on its perch. As soon as it saw Jessica, it gave a loud squawk and flew over to sit on her shoulder.

"Oh, Zebedee," she cried, "Thank goodness you're still here! I thought you'd been sold."

"Polly put the kettle on," the bird replied affectionately.

Mr. Menagerie, the pet shop owner, appeared from the back office. He greeted Jessica with a cheerful smile. "I was hoping you'd stop in today."

"I haven't missed a Saturday yet. But what's going on? Why have you sold everything?"

"I'm off to Africa," Mr. Menagerie said.

"Africa!" Jessica exclaimed.

"My brother, Mr. Lionheart, the famous explorer, has asked me to join him on an expedition."

"Wow! You are lucky," said Jessica. "I've always wanted to have adventures. Nothing exciting ever happens to me."

"You never know when your luck is going to turn," said Mr. Menagerie, mysteriously.

"Whatever do you mean?" asked Jessica.

"Well, I can't take my old friend Zebedee here, and I thought you might like to have him."

"Oh! I'd love to . . . but, I couldn't. I don't have any money."

"I didn't mean buy him." Mr. Menagerie laughed heartily. "I meant to have, as a gift. You visit him so often, and it was you who taught him to talk. Anyway, I'll be glad to know he's gone to a good home."

"I promise I'll look after him properly. Thank you ever so much, Mr. Menagerie, and I do hope you enjoy Africa."

Jessica skipped all the way down the street, across the road and into the Botanical Gardens. Zebedee flew by her side, crying out, "Polly put the kettle on, Polly put the kettle on," and every now and then, "Kettle put the Polly on."

"Before we go home, I shall celebrate this wonderful occasion with a painting," Jessica announced.

Diving into her bag, she pulled out her box of paints, a sketch book, and a little jar of water. Zebedee perched on a low branch and Jessica began. First she chose an indigo blue for the beak and the eye, then a deep crimson for the head. Jessica was careful to leave a spot of white paper in the middle of the eye to give it life. With thick strokes she painted the top half of the body lemon yellow and the rest intense blue with a few red highlights in the tail feathers. Almost finished, she filled in the background with a few leaves and some blue sky. She signed the bottom of the painting with a flourish, "Jessica Tomlins."

"Time to go," said Jessica as she packed up her things. She climbed quickly up the hill with Zebedee perched on her shoulder. It wouldn't do to be late.

Jessica's home was a gloomy building, which huddled in the

shadow of an old office block. The sign outside read "Blackwood Institute for Homeless Young Persons." That was a fancy name. Most people called it an orphanage.

Just as Jessica stepped into the hallway, a door flew open and a tall, bony woman stalked out.

Madame Iceberg had colorless hair scraped back into a bun. Her skin was paper white, which was a shocking contrast to the vicious red color she had painted on her lips and nails.

"Good afternoon, Madame," said Jessica nervously.

"Tomlins," screeched Madame Iceberg (no one ever used first names at the orphanage), "what is that thing on your head?"

"It's Zebedee, my parrot. He was given to me by the pet shop owner."

Madame Iceberg placed her hands on her hips and hissed through long white teeth. "This is a charitable institution. A narrow bed, plain food, and hard work are what we generously provide for you. We do not have luxuries here. We do not have pets. In particular, we do not have dirty and disgusting old birds."

Jessica quivered before the towering form, but she was stubborn and not about to give in easily. She forced herself to meet Madame Iceberg's steely blue eyes. "He won't cost you anything, and he won't be any trouble."

"You're dead right he won't be any trouble, you silly little girl," snarled

Madame Iceberg, angry that Jessica had dared to answer back. "You're going to take him back right this minute."

"I will not," said Jessica, blinking back tears. "And anyway, I can't. Mr. Menagerie will be on his way to Africa by now."

"Then I'll get rid of him. Give him here and I'll wring his neck for you."

Madame Iceberg reached out to snatch Zebedee, who promptly leaned forward and gave her hand a sharp nip. Madame Iceberg let out a screech and leaped back, waving her bleeding hand. Zebedee, frightened by the noise, flew around and around the hallway, squawking, before flying out the open door.

Jessica took one look at Madame Iceberg's furious face and bolted after him.

CHAPTER TWO

With Zebedee flying overhead, Jessica raced down the street and into the Botanical Gardens. She ran past the tea house, out by the cemetery, and down the steep road that led to the middle of the city. She hurried past the tall buildings that jostled each other for space and sunshine, and only slowed down when she reached the harbor.

"You really mustn't bite people, even if they are being nasty," Jessica scolded Zebedee, who had perched on her shoulder. "I wouldn't have let her hurt you."

"Poor Polly! Poor, poor Polly," Zebedee crooned softly.

"We have to think what we are going to do. We can't go back to the orphanage, that's for sure. You'd be fed to the cat. No, what we've got to do is make our own way in the world and have a few adventures, too. Just like Mr. Menagerie."

They wandered along the harbor until they reached the wharves, where lots of ships were anchored. Jessica stopped to look at a strange ship tied up to the jetty. It had a large, square sail with patches on it. "What a wicked-looking ship," said Jessica. "I bet it belongs to some pirates. Look, here's the name, *The Black Mischief*, and there's a note tied to the mooring rope."

WANTED: ONE CABIN PERSON FOR LONG & DANGEROUS VOYAGE APPLY WITHIN

"This could be just the thing we need," said Jessica excitedly. "A way to escape from Madame Iceberg, travel the world, and have adventures." She looked around, but the ship seemed deserted.

"Excuse me," she called in a timid voice. There was no response. "I'll have to be a bit bolder," she thought. "Ahoy there, anyone on board?" Jessica yelled at the top of her voice.

A black-bearded face with a red scarf and golden earring peered out of a square hole in the side of the ship.

"Ahoy there," yelled Jessica again, waving to attract attention. "I've come to apply for the position of adventurous cabin person."

The bearded face disappeared, and a few seconds later a ramp was lowered from the side of the vessel. Feeling very brave, Jessica walked up the narrow piece of wood. She was careful not to look down in case she wobbled and fell into the water. As she stepped up on deck, she was greeted by the bearded face, which turned out to belong to a jolly man dressed in purple-spotted trousers and a green and yellow silk shirt. He beamed at Jessica and winked one wicked blue eye. The other eye was covered by a black patch.

"Ahoy there, matey, Captain Black-eye Jack at your service, and this here is Mrs. Black-eye Jack, otherwise known as One-legged Rosie."

Jessica turned and shook hands with

a merry woman who had very brown skin, twinkling eyes, and a wide grin that showed one missing front tooth. She wasn't quite as big and hearty as Black-eye Jack, but made up for it by shouting "Ahoy there!" quite a lot and slapping her wooden leg with gusto.

"So then, me hearty, you want to be a cabin person," said Black-eye Jack.

"Yes, sir!" answered Jessica smartly.

"And that there bird would be wanting to fill the position of ship's parrot?"

"Oh, yes! I couldn't go anywhere without Zebedee. After all, he's partly the reason I ran awa . . . that is, er . . . "

"Run away, have ye?" Black-eye

Jack leaned forward and stared at her intently with his wicked, blue eye. Then, to her surprise, he slapped his thigh and roared with laughter. "Ah, you seem a promising sort. Only the best run away to sea. Now, can you scrub decks, sew a torn sail, climb the rigging, and still sing sea chanteys of an evening?"

"Yes, sir," said Jessica. "I've had plenty of practice scrubbing floors and mending clothes at the orphanage. I'm not sure what rigging is, but I'm very good at climbing trees, and I'm always getting told off for singing to myself."

"Well, you do sound like a likely lass. Welcome aboard, Cabin Person Jessica. Your wages will be a gold coin each month and a share in any treasure we find," said Black-eye Jack.

"And here are some proper clothes," cried Rosie. "We can't have a jolly cabin person dressed in an orphanage uniform."

Gleefully, Jessica gave her drab black pinafore and gray shirt to Rosie. Then she slipped on the blue striped trousers and baggy yellow shirt, and tied up her long hair with a green scarf.

"That's much better! I feel like I've forgotten the orphanage already," she declared.

By the time evening arrived and the moon had risen over the city, they were ready to leave. For the first half hour, Jessica was very busy. She rushed around tightening this and loosening that as Black-eye Jack shouted instructions.

Zebedee perched on the ship's bell and squawked the alarm if he thought they were sailing too close to other ships.

At last they left the harbor, and the open sea beckoned before them. The waves swelled joyously, the clouds chased each other across the starlit sky, and the deck heaved up and down. Unfortunately, Jessica's stomach heaved with it. First she turned a dead white and then a bright green, and then she rushed to the side of the ship to be sick.

"Oh dear, oh dear," cried One-legged Rosie, rushing up to her. "I think you'd better go and lie on your bunk for tonight and nibble some dry ship's biscuits. Perhaps you'll have found your sea legs by morning."

Jessica thought that it wasn't sea legs she needed so much as a sea stomach. She had never felt so sick in all her life.

All night she tossed and turned in her narrow bunk bed, and nothing and no one could comfort her, not even Zebedee, who perched on the end of the bed muttering, "Poor Polly." The next day she was no better—if anything, she felt worse. By lunch time Jessica felt so terrible, she declared she wanted to die.

"I can see we're going to have to take you back to land," said Rosie.

They sailed into the very next town that was spotted along the coast. Jessica hurried down the gangplank to the jetty, relieved to be standing on something that didn't buck around underneath her.

"Goodbye, Captain Black-eye Jack. Goodbye, One-legged Rosie," she cried. "I'm sorry I turned out to be unseaworthy."

"Don't you worry, lass," said One-legged Rosie kindly. "It can happen to the best of us. You can keep those clothes. The others were only fit for cleaning rags. And here is a piece of treacle tart and some nuts for Zebedee."

"Farewell, me hearty," cried Black-eye Jack, slapping Jessica heartily on the shoulder.

CHAPTER THREE

Jessica and Zebedee watched until *The Black Mischief* had sailed out of sight. They then wandered through the town until they found a park. They sat under a shady chestnut tree, and soon Jessica began to feel better.

She was still feeling sad at parting from her new friends, though, and decided it would be a good idea to paint some pictures to help her remember them.

First of all, she painted portraits of Black-eye Jack wearing his pirate's hat and One-legged Rosie dancing a jig. Finally, she painted *The Black Mischief* rolling on the waves.

Just as the paintings had finished drying, Jessica noticed a long line of trucks driving into the park. They stopped in a large playing field nearby. "Vanessa Feather's Famous Flying Circus," Jessica read out from the side of each truck. "Just think, Zebedee. If we could join the circus, we would be able to travel the world and have adventures without having to set foot on a ship."

"Polly put the kettle on," agreed Zebedee.

Once the men had finished putting up the big top, Jessica and Zebedee crawled under the side of the tent. Inside, two children were doing an acrobatic act. Jessica crouched down behind some seats to watch. The children flew through the air like great wingless birds, swooping and diving, soaring and wheeling, dancing on the air as if there was no such thing as gravity and broken bones.

With the boldness of a pirate, Jessica marched up to them. "Hello," she said, "My name's Jessica, and this is Zebedee. We thought your act was fantastic, and we'd like to join your circus and learn how to be acrobats."

"It looks like your parrot has already started his training," the boy laughed, pointing up to where Zebedee was perched high on the swinging seat.

"Hi, I'm Shula," said the girl. "Mom's just coming over. She's the ringmaster. You'll have to talk to her if you want to join us."

Vanessa Feather was a tall, slim woman with very long black hair.

She listened thoughtfully as Jessica told her of her plans.

"Well, Jessica," she said eventually, "we'd be delighted to teach you to be an acrobat if you seem good at it. Why don't you have a try on the swing now, since everything is already set up?"

Jessica gave Zebedee to Shula and bravely started up the ladder. She looked only at the next rung and never down at the floor, just as One-legged Rosie had taught her when climbing the rigging of the ship. It seemed like a long time before she reached the little platform at the top of the pole. The next part was a lot more difficult because she had to let go of the pole in order to reach the side of the swing.

Even though she knew the safety net was waiting to catch her if she fell, her heart still pounded and her forehead glistened with sweat. She carefully inched her way across the platform and took hold of the swing. Sitting down, she hooked her legs over the bar, grabbed the ropes and pushed off.

At first it was a wonderful feeling to be swinging high up in the roof of the big top. Then she looked down. She was so far up, the people looked like toy dolls, and Zebedee was no more than a speck of red. The floor seemed to swim up to meet her, and everything became a blur. Quickly, Jessica closed her eyes to keep herself from fainting and clung tightly to the swing. She could hear the others yelling helpful things from down below.

"Move your legs back and forth—you'll swing higher that way."

"Let go with your arms and see if you can hang upside down."

Eventually she heard someone say, "I think she's stuck."

"Jessica, just let go and fall into the net."

"It's perfectly safe; pretend you're a bird."

Finally, she heard light steps coming up the ladder, and the swing move gently as Shula slipped on beside her. She gently released Jessica's hands from the swing, and together they swooped down into the waiting net.

"I'm ever so sorry," said Jessica,

when she had stopped shaking.

"Now, don't worry, you never know if you can do something until you try. I'm afraid the problem is that you are too old to learn to be an acrobat," said Vanessa.

"Too old!" Jessica exclaimed. "But I'm only ten."

"Exactly. Shula could perform a triple back twist when she was only two, and Marc learned to walk on the tightrope before he could walk on the ground. To be a good acrobat, you really have to be born in the circus and start then."

"Oh! I see."

"Don't be too sad. Why don't you stay with us for a while. There are always plenty of things to do on the ground."

"I thought you did really well even to make it onto the swing," Marc said kindly.

"Pretty Polly," Zebedee agreed.

Jessica stayed with the circus while it was in town. She helped out by mending costumes, putting up posters that advertised shows, and generally fetching and carrying. Zebedee was given a little part in the clown's routine in which he would imitate the ringmaster's voice and have the audience in fits of laughter. During the quiet times, Jessica painted pictures of her new friends—Corky the clown, Firenzo the fire eater and, of course, Shula and Marc.

At last it was time for the circus to leave. Jessica and Zebedee felt very sad as they watched the trucks disappear into the distance. Since it was raining, Jessica decided to go into the shopping mall, where it was warm, and cheer herself and Zebedee up with a chocolate bun and some nuts. They settled themselves down on a bench, and Jessica took out her paintings to remind them of the friends they had made since they left the orphanage.

"I don't know, Zebedee—how are we going to make our way in the world when I can't go to sea because I get seasick and I'm too old to be an acrobat?"

As Jessica and Zebedee sat lost in thought, a crowd gathered around the pictures.

"I'll have that one, Dearie," a voice

said. "The one of the pirate with the patch. He reminds me of my brother Jake, who ran away to sea twenty years ago. How much?"

"Oh it isn't for . . ." began Jessica, and then she noticed the crowd. Suddenly she had a wonderful idea. "Ten dollars," she said boldly.

"I'll take it," said the woman and handed over a crisp bill.

It seemed that everyone wanted a picture. Lots of children had been to the circus and wanted a picture of their favorite act. An old lady took a liking to the portraits of Zebedee and bought two, and a young man wanted the portrait of One-legged Rosie because it reminded him of his mother. Soon Jessica had no pictures left, but she did have quite a lot of money.

"Look at this," she cried. "We can make our way in the world and have adventures after all."

And that is exactly what Jessica and Zebedee did. Together they trekked across the Sahara desert on a camel, sailed down the Amazon river in a canoe, and went on walkabout with the Aborigines in Australia. Wherever they went, Jessica painted what she had seen. Her paintings were so full of life, so bright and cheerful and exciting, that everyone wanted to buy them, and she became quite famous.

Zebedee also became famous in his own way, for he learned to sing "Polly Put the Kettle On" in fourteen different languages and was asked to appear on talk shows and to open school fairs. They never stayed in the same place for long, however. The call of new experiences and new friends was always too strong, and off they would go to see what the next adventure would bring.